Terrible Tim!

by
KATIE HAWORTH

illustrated by
LAURA HUGHES

little bee books

Terrible Tim likes to

Terrible Tim likes to R O

Terrible Tim
likes to
DASH.

Terrible Tim
likes to

SPLAS

DRAW

ROAR

DASH

SPLASH
Terrible,
terrible
Tim!

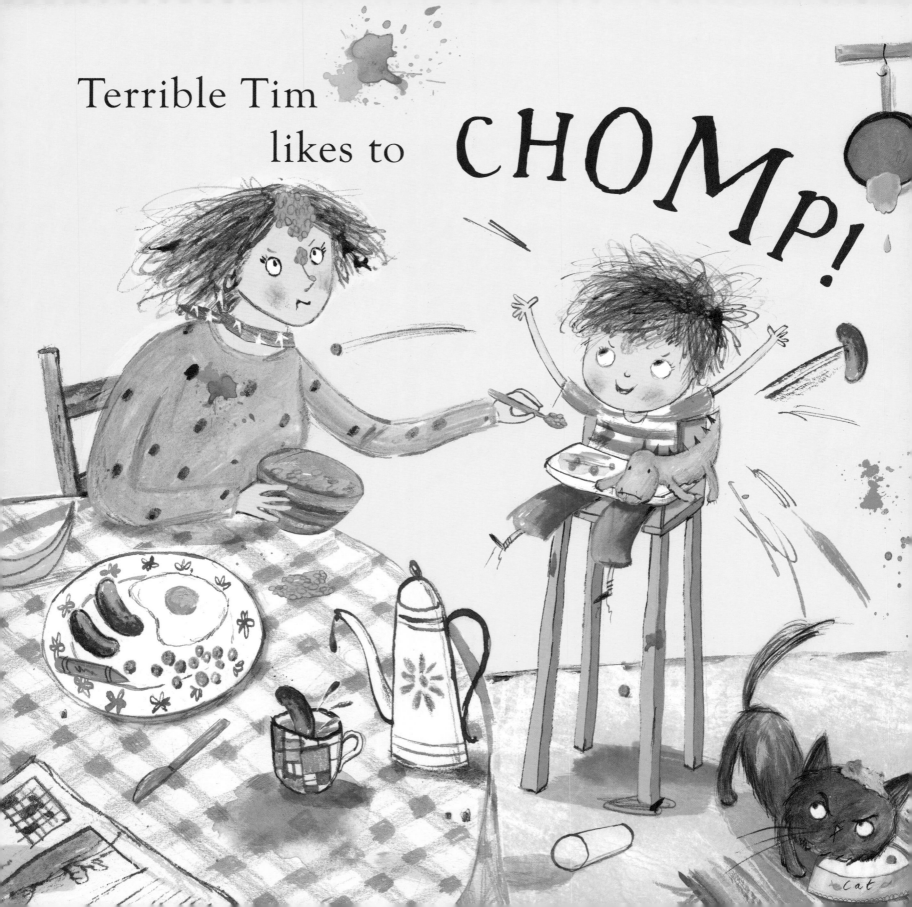

Terrible Tim
likes to
CHOMP!

Terrible Tim likes to
STOMP!

Terrible Tim
likes to

Terrible Tim
likes to

CHOMP

STOMP

MAKE

BREAK

Terrible Tim
LIKES to

cuddle.

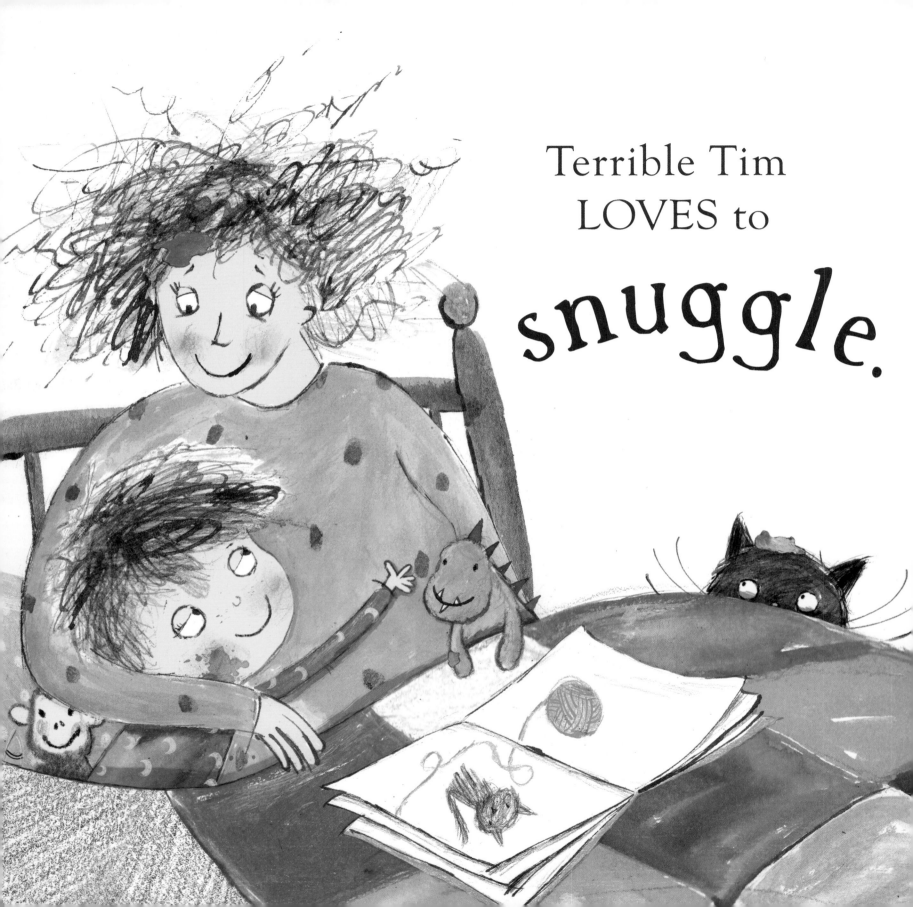

Terrible Tim
LOVES to
snuggle.

Night, night,
sleep tight . . .

Tim!

For Timmi who isn't
terrible at all, and who
built MW with
his bare hands

L.H.

For Archie, who
was the original
Tim, and for Thea,
who will be the
second if her mad
aunt has anything
to do with it

K.H.

little bee books

A division of Bonnier Publishing
853 Broadway, New York, New York 10003
Designed by Verity Clark
Written by Katie Haworth
Edited by Alison Ritchie
Text and design © 2016 by The Templar Company Limited
Illustrations © 2016 by Laura Hughes
This little bee books edition, 2016.
All rights reserved, including the right of
reproduction in whole or in part in any form.
LITTLE BEE BOOKS is a trademark of Bonnier Publishing
Group, and associated colophon is a trademark of
Bonnier Publishing Group.
Manufactured in China 0080316
First Edition 2 4 6 8 10 9 7 5 3 1

Library of Congress Cataloging-in-Publication Data
is available upon request.
ISBN 978-1-4998-0137-8
littlebeebooks.com
bonnierpublishing.com